Welcome to The Giggle Club

The Giggle Club is a collection of picture books made to put a giggle into early reading. There are funny stories about a contrary mouse, a dancing fox, a turtle with a trumpet, a pig with a ball, a hungry monster, a laughing lobster, an elephant who sneezes away the jungle and lots more! Each of these characters is a member of **The Giggle Club**, but anyone can join: just pick up a **Giggle Club** book, read it and get giggling!

Turn to the checklist on the inside back cover and tick off the Giggle Club books you have read.

TEE HEE!

HA HA!

*For Oskar, Joe next door
and Tiziana* ~ J.B-B.

First published 1998 by Walker Books Ltd
87 Vauxhall Walk, London SE11 5HJ

10 9 8 7 6 5 4 3

Text © 1998 Martin Waddell
Illustrations © 1998 John Bendall-Brunello

This book has been typeset in Horley.

Printed in Hong Kong

British Library Cataloguing in Publication Data
A catalogue record for this book is
available from the British Library.

ISBN 0-7445-5478-0

Yum, Yum, Yummy

written by

Martin Waddell

illustrated by

John Bendall~Brunello

WALKER BOOKS
AND SUBSIDIARIES
LONDON • BOSTON • SYDNEY

One day three little bears went off to the Honey~bee Tree to get honey for Mummy.

Guzzley was there
but the three little bears
didn't see Guzzley Bear.

The three little
bears filled their
pots with honey.
Then they set off
for home.

Greedy Guzzley was there
but the three little bears
didn't see Guzzley Bear.

"Grr-grr-grr!"
growled Guzzley Bear.
"Give me your honey!"

Yum,
yum,
yummy!
The honey went
into Guzzley's
big tummy.

Three scared little bears ran
all the way home.

"Guzzley Bear stole our honey,"
they told their mummy.

"Don't be scared, little bears,"
said Mummy. "You go for
more honey. I'll see to
that old Guzzley Bear."

The three little bears went back to the Honey~bee Tree. Guzzley Bear crept up behind them. Mummy was there but Guzzley Bear didn't see Mummy Bear.

"**Grr-grr-grr!**"
growled Guzzley Bear,
"Give me your honey!"
But out of the
bushes came ...

Guzzley Bear never
came back any more.
The honey went into three
little bear tummies ...

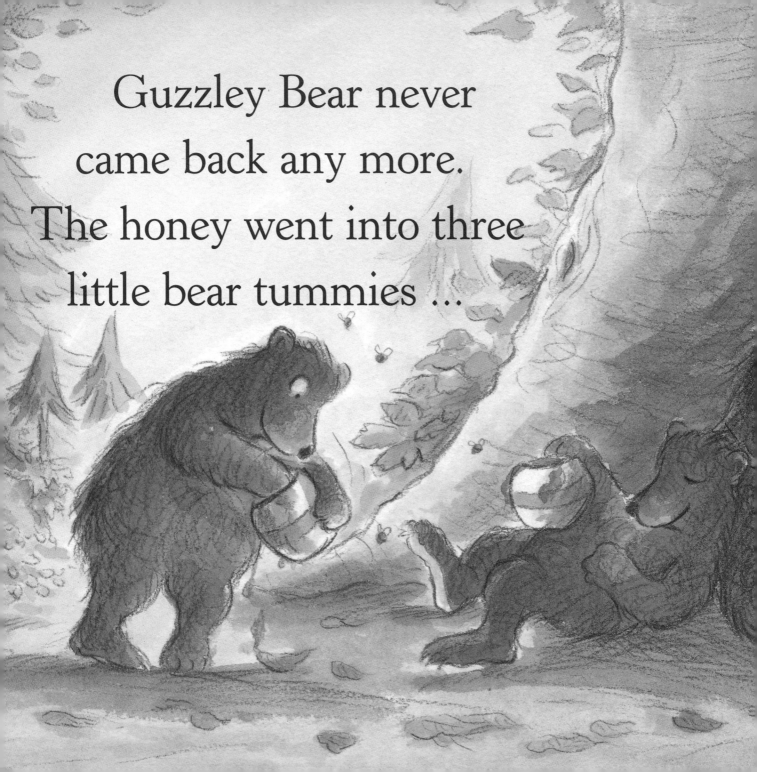

and Mummy's.
Yum,
yum,
yum,
yummy!

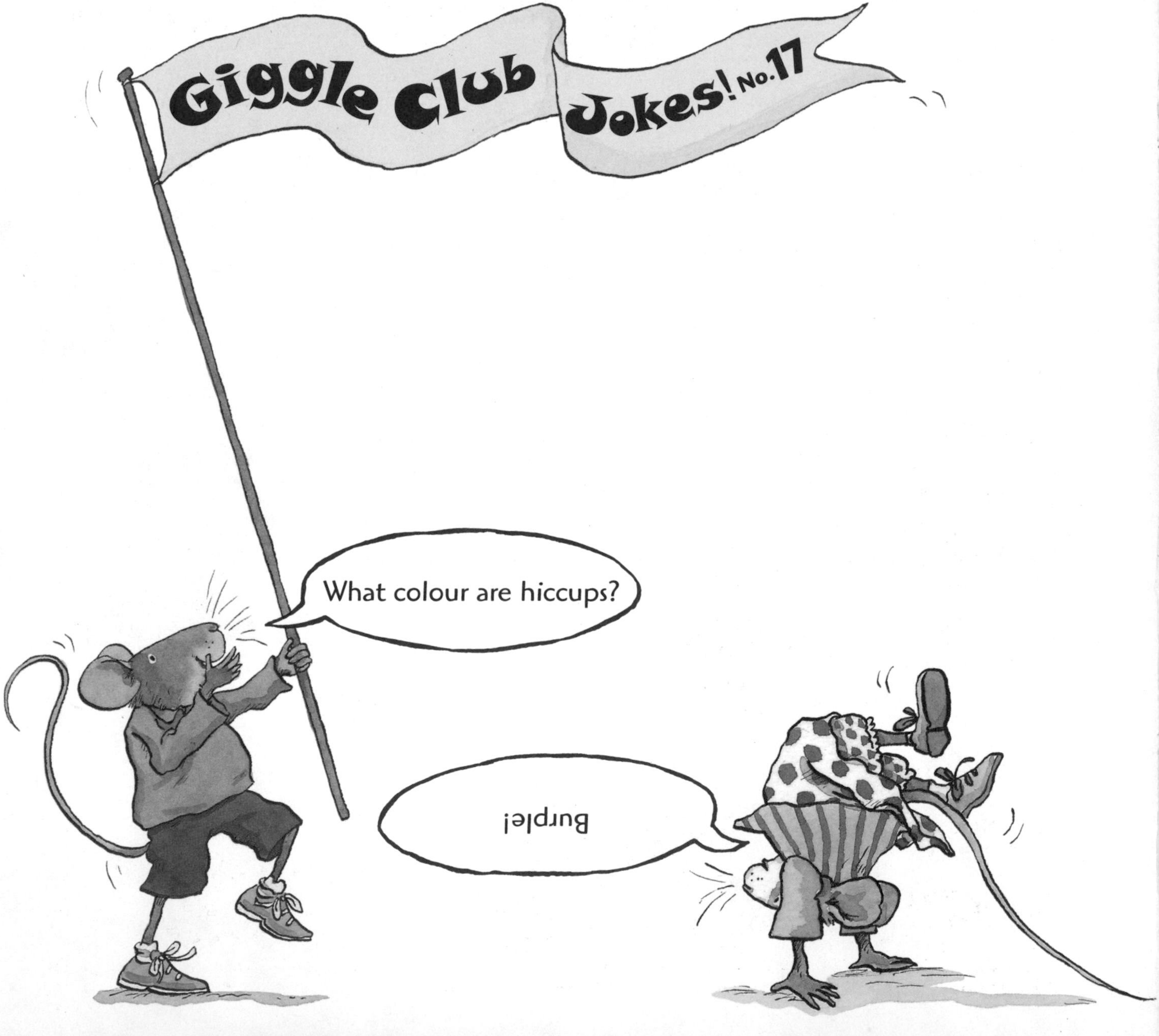
Giggle Club Jokes! No.17
What colour are hiccups?
Burple!